# Peter Cottontail

## And the Great Mitten Hunt

**By Laura Norton**
**Illustrated by Linda Karl**

A GOLDEN BOOK • NEW YORK
Golden Books Publishing Company, Inc., New York, New York 10106

 Library of Congress Catalog Card Number: 98-83006 ISBN: 0-307-16007-6 A MCMXCIX First Edition 1999

It was the day before Easter and everyone in April Valley was very excited. All year long, they had dyed eggs and made Easter baskets. Finally, everyone could rest.

Everyone, that is, but Peter Cottontail.

Peter Cottontail was the Chief Easter Bunny. It was his job to deliver all of the baskets and hide all of the eggs for all of the Easter egg hunts in the world.

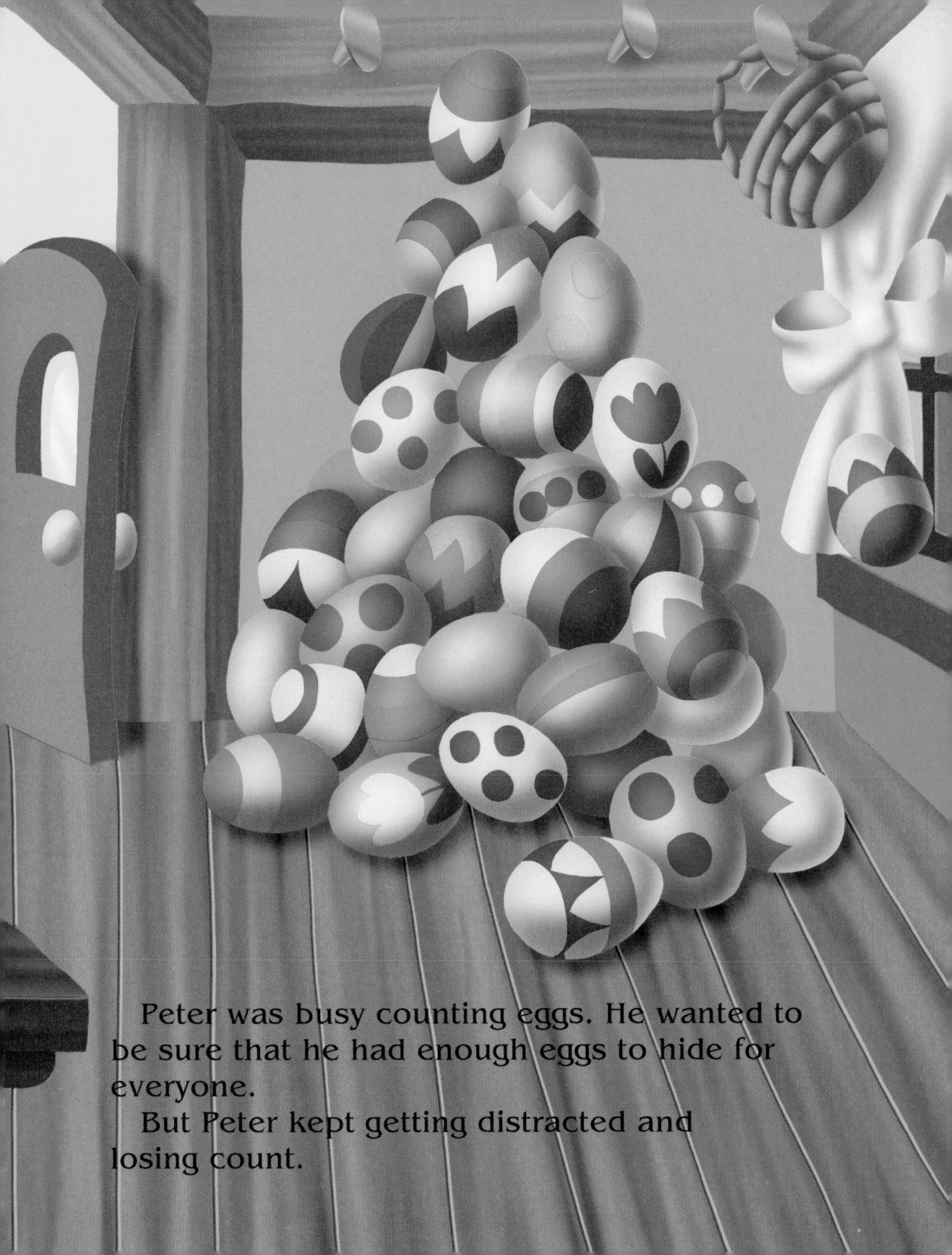

Peter was busy counting eggs. He wanted to be sure that he had enough eggs to hide for everyone.

But Peter kept getting distracted and losing count.

First, Peter thought that he heard the *meow* of one little kitten. But he didn't see any kittens, so he started to count again.

Then Peter thought that he heard two *meows* from two little kittens. But he still didn't see anything.

When Peter heard the sound of three *meows* from three little kittens, he decided to investigate.

He searched under eggs and behind baskets—still no kittens.

"Maybe they're outside," thought Peter. So, he opened the door and sure enough...

There sat three very unhappy little kittens.

"What's wrong, little kittens?" asked Peter.

"We were playing hide-and-seek with our mittens," explained the three little kittens. "We are very good at hiding, but we are not very good at seeking. And now our mittens are lost."

The three little kittens who lost their mittens began to cry.

Peter wanted to help, but there was still so much to do for Easter. Then Peter had an idea.

"If you'll help me count my eggs, then I can help you find your mittens," he told them.

The three little kittens were so happy that they began to dance and sing.

Everyone went into the house and, one-two-three, they counted all of the eggs. There were eggs enough for everyone and even three too many.

"Great!" said Peter. "It's good to have extra eggs, just in case any break. Now let's go find your mittens."

Off went Peter Cottontail and the three little kittens, with Peter hopping big bunny hops and the kittens racing along to keep up.

First, they passed a house made of straw—but no one was home.

Next, they passed a house made of sticks. No one was home there either.

Finally, they came to a very nice house made of bricks.

Peter and the kittens knocked on the door of the pretty brick house and three little pigs came out to meet them.

"Welcome! Welcome!" said the three little pigs. "We are so glad to have visitors. The Big Bad Wolf chased all of our friends away and no one visits us anymore. Won't you come in for a little while?"

Peter and the kittens explained that they were looking for the kittens' lost mittens. This made the kittens so sad that they began to cry again.

"Don't cry little kittens," said the three little pigs. "We haven't seen any mittens, but you are welcome to look around."

So everyone looked around, but they didn't find any mittens.

"You should ask the old woman who lives in a shoe," suggested the three little pigs. "Maybe she has seen your mittens."

Peter and the kittens thanked the pigs and said goodbye and down the road they went.

Before long, they came to an old woman standing near to a giant shoe. There were children running everywhere.

The children were making so much noise that the kittens had to shout.

"HAVE YOU SEEN OUR MITTENS?"

"NO," yelled the old woman as loud as she could. "BUT MAYBE THE CHILDREN HAVE!"

She pulled out a shiny whistle and gave a mighty blow. Suddenly, the children were silent.

"These poor kittens have lost their mittens," said the old woman. "Has anyone seen them?"

The children had not seen the mittens. "But we will help you look," they offered.

Everyone searched all around the giant shoe. They found hats and socks and gloves and scarves, but they didn't find any mittens.

"You should ask Humpty Dumpty," suggested the old woman. "He sits so high up on his wall that he sees everything."

Peter and the kittens thanked the old woman and her children and said goodbye. Then off they went, with Peter hopping big bunny hops and the kittens racing along to keep up.

Before long, they came to a very, very high wall, with a strange little man sitting on top.

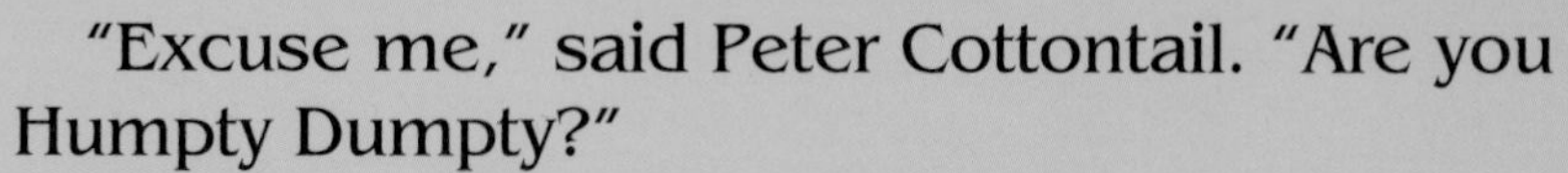

"Excuse me," said Peter Cottontail. "Are you Humpty Dumpty?"

The man looked down from the top of his very, very high wall.

"Yes, I am," said the man. "How can I help you?"

Once again, the three little kittens explained how they had lost their mittens. And they became so sad that, once again, they began to cry.

"Do not cry, little kittens," said Humpty Dumpty. "This morning, I saw three little kittens carefully hide their mittens in the tall grass next to the Babbling Brook."

The three little kittens began to dance and sing.

"Now we remember! Thank you, thank you!" they cried.

Peter was very happy to have helped the kittens. But suddenly, he remembered about Easter.

"Oh no!" he cried. "It is almost Easter and I haven't delivered the baskets or hidden the eggs. What will I do?"

"Don't worry," said the three little kittens. "You have seen that we are good at hiding things. While you deliver the Easter baskets, we will hide the eggs."

Peter accepted their help and off everyone rushed, with Peter hopping big bunny hops and the kittens racing along to keep up.

By Easter morning everything was finished. Best of all, none of the eggs had broken, so Peter gave the three beautiful extra eggs to the three little kittens as thanks for all of their help.